HOMEGIRL AIN'T GONNA MAKE IT

1

ERIC REESE

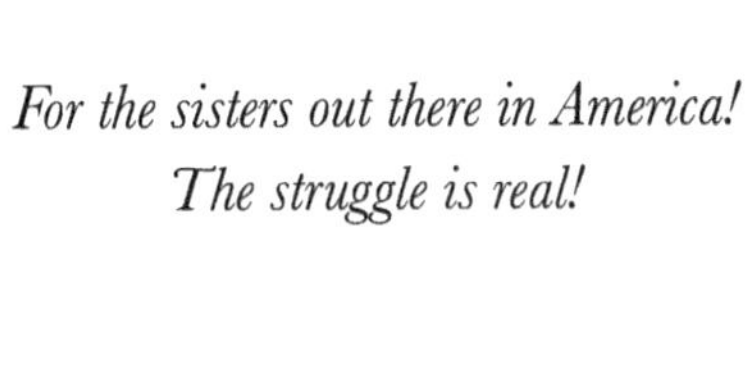

For the sisters out there in America!
The struggle is real!

CONTENTS

1

The hotel room was dark even though the windows were open, and the blinds pulled aside. The moon was probably somewhere huddled up and covering itself with a cloud blanket, having abandoned her place in the sky. The skies looked like they were turning in for the night, so they can get their own sleep. Outside, on the streets of Boston, horns announced the movement of cars. Their owners were sleepless and the footsteps could be heard, but the sound didn't reach where I was staying.

My name is Gabrielle. If you saw me sprawled on the carpet, with all these papers scattered around me, you'd think I was dead. I was exhausted from the long travel from New York to Boston. The slow rising and falling of my chest and my eyes pointed I was fast asleep. Sleep had come upon me sudden-like, robbing the papers I had in my company and dragging me along into its comfy walls. Coffee was on the table, untouched, now having gone cold from sitting out. I wanted to stay up to do some research, but that's not happening tonight. My suitcase was watching me from the top of the table where I had left it, unpacked.

A movement, unnoticeable at first, then quietly forming into a silhouette stirred just outside the window. My eyes sprang open. For seconds, I was staring into a pair of eyes looking in on me from another building's window, then there was nothing. I tried getting up to investigate, but my legs had something else in mind. They collapsed near the bed while my eyes strayed uneasily to the window where there was nothing. The deception of the eyes, I thought without really thinking. Sleep patted my head and pampered me straight into unconsciousness again.

"Beep, beep, beep…"

I groaned and rolled over. The alarm sound continued and my hand searched for the terrorist that seemed to scream louder, the more frantic my movements became.

"Where…"

"Beep, beep, beep, beep…"

"… are you?"

The alarm would not ceasefire until either I get up or realize I was dreaming. The clock sat on a shelf above the bed. I got myself together and turned it off.

"Damn. It's early."

I fell back into the bed as my long black hair cascaded down the length of my back.

"I'm so beat," I murmured into the bedsheet.

The bed seemed to hear me and sank me further. With great effort, I rolled away from that magnetic comfort and grabbed my watch off the bed desk. It was 7: 15 am.

"Oh shit! I'm gonna be late." I hurried, scrambling out of the bed.

I was scheduled to come in by 8. Can a sister get a good break in my life, sometime? I'm tired, but it is what it is. The Greyhound got into Boston 11 hours ago and had stayed up most of the night trying to find out ways to impress my new employers. This will be my first real job and I'd be damned if I would let it slip away.

Forty-five minutes was such a short time to get ready. If I did not get going, I'd be late and jobless. Quickly, I went to the bathroom, pulled the door shut and had the shower running in no time. The hot water running down my smooth ebony skin did more than wash me. I felt the fatigue leaving me like it was evaporating. I let myself be drawn to the person staring back at me from the bathroom mirror.

Some say I have a nice body. *Never mind that.* My long natural lashes lined up on the sides of a pair of big eyes, which still looked tired albeit the shower. There were the faint rings around my eyes, but they did nothing to fault the perfect combination those big eyes made with my little nose and my perfectly carved full lips. Even the cynic in me had to admit that I was beautiful and that those eyes could melt a lion's heart. I let my eyes travel down the length of my body, my firm perky breasts and the curve of my hips that began with such subtlety at the waist I kept looking at it, trying to figure out how it had become. I snatched my eyes from the mirror before it traveled down my legs to you know where. I knew what was coming next and did not have time. My hands were already past my navel. I pulled them off my body, closing my eyes and breathing in deeply. When I opened them, I sensed eyes still running over my body and glanced into the mirror. My reflection's eyes were slow in returning to match mine.

2

Detective Gibbons of Boston PD let the car engine run idly for a while he searched for his partner among the hustle and bustle of Boston's streets. The fool could have just stayed home and let his partner come to carry him, but he was afraid he would meet his girlfriend. *Why would someone be afraid of his partner meeting his girlfriend, anyway?* The insecure bastard, Gibbons thought with some fondness. Maybe if he had not teased him so much, he would have met this queen he had heard so much about. No biggy. *Why do his friends think he was always after their girls?* Okay, maybe the detective was too much of a flirt, but that made his job easier. Sometimes all he had to do was get next to the lady, stare at her and information would come tumbling out from the unlikeliest places. *"Just things I do for my country,"* was *Gibbon's motto.* The patriotism he had for America made his views sometimes conflict with his colleagues.

On the other hand, Detective Pete wouldn't share his view with him, of course. He would scrunch up his face to show how disgusting he thought it was, which was very disgusting. Pete was a baby in a man's body and often believed too much, he heard.

Detective Gibbons' stomach grumbled and rumbled. He winced. He had to eat something before the day began facing grotesque picture after grotesque picture of dead people; good, bad, small, big, smart and stupid. He became known for the case of a man trying to take on three armed gangsters single-handedly. Of course, Gibbons quickly became local history but felt a little guilty. He was also stupid, so it was really hypocritical of him calling anyone stupid. He had done stupid things before this, and had scars to remind him of just how stupid he had been in the line of duty.

The passenger door was pulled open and Pete jumped in.

"Hey, bud."

"Hey," Gibbons replied, smiling. Not

seeing Pete come up. For a brief second, he wondered what he would have done if it were some hoodlum, thug, gangsta or whatever name he could label a black. *Is that not how it always happening? A career detective who had been a thorn in the flesh of criminals meeting his death at the hands of an insignificant posse member. What if it was one of those criminals pulling the trigger?*

"You okay, Gib?"

"Yeah, man. Just daydreaming"

Damn, Gib's been watching too many movies. He even forgot he hates being called Gib, it sounded like glib. Could Pete not think of something better?

"You don't look good."

"I don't?"

"Breakfast?"

"No," Gibbons replied, "had to wait too long for your lame ass. "

"Too early, Gibbons, too early."

"Early or not, the ass is lame if it is lame."

"Can we get moving?"

"Sire," Gibbons snickered and shifted the gear to drive.

"How's the missus?"

"She's fine."

"Is she as sneaky and dodgy as you?"

"We're a fine match."

"Hmm. Sounds like someone's trying to convince himself."

"You wish."

"Tell you what, Pete. You and your mistress, just you two should come for dinner at my house."

Gibbons saw the now-forming smile on Pete's face.

"Thanks, but no thanks. I'll take a raincheck."

"We live in a fucking democracy, Pete. We haven't asked the lady yet."

"And we're not going to."

"You're saying she has no say?"

"Not in this."

"Bloody chauvinist. "

"Watch the road ahead, remember you're driving."

Gibbons smiled as he maneuvered the squad car through the streets, past early morning pedestrians hurrying to catch the train. The traffic was slowly building up on the main road and some shops that hadn't stayed open through the night had 'open' signs hung at the entrance. Today would be a tough one, Gibbons felt.

"You know, Pete, you can tell me her name. It's not like we can find a woman with that name. Haha."

"Okay."

"So, what is it? Mary? Jane? Brienne? Arya? Anika? Keisha. You look like someone that should be dating someone named Anne."

"Really?"

"Yeah, I know these kinds of things."

"Of course, you do partner. So who were you with last night? Anne? Annabel? Susan? Beth? Sasha…"

"Gwen. I was with Gwen."

"Gee, who would have thought?"

"She's hot, man. I can still feel her mouth on my cock."

"Can you please save me that bullshit this morning?"

"I will but what's her name?"

"Oh gee, we're here. The food dump."

———

Gibbons found a place to park, then jumped out after Pete. Their clothes fit in perfectly. Gibs didn't feel the usual hairs rising on the back of his neck when he walked through the doorway. Few people paid them attention. It wasn't like they were famous. They hurried their breakfast, so they could get back to work.

As usual, Pete's little eyes were all over the place at once, probing, searching, suspecting. He hated being caught unaware. Yes, Pete did. The first time both of them had ever been caught unaware when he got that nasty scar across his abdomen. He had already asked God to forgive his sins before he realized he wasn't dead.

Pete found them a table at the far left corner where they could watch the entire restaurant. Gibbons ordered a hamburger and a milkshake while Pete had ice cream.

"What the hell? Really man, that's fucking breakfast for you?" Gibbons bursted out.

"I've already had something at home."

"What about a burger?"

"Oh, Touché."

Gibbons bit into his hamburger while his mind wandered away from the restaurant. His eyes looked sad as he pondered on the possibility of leaving his partner and his friend. It was a funny thought, but that was all the thought he had this morning. Gwen from last night was a lie he had made up, so there was nothing to savor from the past day. He would never admit this to Pete, but he stayed up all night thinking about how different things would be if he had a permanent relationship and not just the flings, one-night-stands and romps in Boston's darkest hallways. There was just no one to fill in that empty void in him that he tried covering with the playboy act, the overflowing sexual euphemisms and innuendos. Gibbons was born to live this way or as he thought. Again, he went back to his favorite motto but this time saying it out loud - *things I do for my country*.

"What was that?" asked Pete, eyes narrowed, staring at him.

"What was what?" Gibbons asked as he took a bite of his hamburger.

"Things you do for your country?"

"Oh, I said that out loud?"

Pete looked him again.

"You sure you're okay?"

"I am, Pete. What's this girl turning you into? A fussy hen? I'm okay, grandpa."

Pete said nothing for a few moments as he finished eating his ice cream.

"Well, hurry up, we have to get going."

Pete stood up and went to the men's room. Gibbons watched him go as his teeth sank into the hamburger again.

"Dispatch, 26 Broadway, Boston. A man has been found dead in his office, second floor. Injuries to the neck. The culprit is on the loose."

"Roger that," said Gibbons trying to understand what he said.

"What's this mumble jumble?" sighed Gibbons as he got up to get Pete.

3

———

I flagged down a taxi outside of The Owls Hills Hotel where I had stayed for the night. I would be late and that would be a terrible first impression to make.

"50 Broadway Street."

"Aye," the taxi driver replied zooming off.

Could this taxi go any faster? I sat hoping it would. I was a little fidgety and had to get a hold of myself before I reached the new startup company that had hired me. Now, that was where the problem laid; I was finding it difficult to find a worthy job even through I had an Ivy League University degree. Man, I was one of the top students back two years ago, racking up academic awards here and there to the envy of the other students and the admiration of my lecturers. But with all that, I still didn't deem myself worthy of being among the best. Post-graduation realities had caught up with my delicate self-esteem as I messed up interview after interview. I gave the interviewers reasons to send my black ass through the door. There were different doors shut before me, but I rejected the taboo it was because I was black at first, anyway.

Not all of my work histories had been sad songs. I got some part-time jobs in retail where my low self-esteem didn't bother me; leaving me stuttering at the easiest of questions. The random duties frustrated me though. They were not what I had in mind as I walked through the hallways of my alma mater, setting out to be the best I could be.

Now, I was brought here to Boston, Massachusetts for a fresh start. This new company called Revival impressed me. They wanted young talent to expand their brand by doing social media branding and promotional advertising in-person. *Didn't sound hard for 60K a year?* Somehow, I'd kept it together this one time alone, focusing on being the persona I showed everyone back in school. So it is, Boston. I wouldn't feel homesick I believed. The town had the same hustle and

bustle that made New York, New York ex-
cept for one thing; diversity. There were
many stories from some of my girls back in
NY about the racial epitomes of the city. I
told them let me see for myself.

———

My phone rang as the driver culled around a
bend, expertly straightening out the steering
wheel after he was done making the turn.

"Hello, Ummi. Salam alaikum."

"Wa alaikum as Salam, Gabrielle, did
you sleep well?"

"Nope, but I tried. I woke up late."

I whispered the word 'late' like I did not
want the cab driver to hear.

"Oh dear, where are you now?"

"In a taxi, on my way to work."

"Did you make your prayers this
morning?"

"Come on, mom."

"You should, always, always—" Ummi
kept repeating 'always' like it had some sort
of enticing quality to her.

"Okay, I will. Gotta go, Ummi, I'm almost at work."

"May Allah protect you."

"Ameen."

I said "Ameen" as a matter of obligation and dutifulness to my mom. Ummi and Abee were devoutly religious. Thankfully, none of their extremities had rubbed off on me and my sister Khadi. I was a think-tank who seldom dealt in sentiments.

"We're here, ma'am."

I was almost sure there was relish in his voice even as I felt my heart palpitate. *"Breath in deeply, girl. You got this."*

I paid the cab driver and got out at a one-story building which had the name of "Revival" engraved on it. *A start-up, eh? Is that what they call it these days to be able to negotiate favorable wages for themselves?* I stood staring at the entrance and envision myself at my desk and before I could see further, a loud honk had woke me out of my daydream.

"Deep breath, deep breath. You're a strong black woman. You can do this," I told myself.

My legs moved slowly and sped up more and more as I got closer to the entrance. My palms were sweaty as I glanced at my watch reading 7:55 AM. I made it in early. Al hamdulilah, perhaps I'm worthy of this blessing. I went inside the building to the receptionist's desk.

"Hello, good morning. Excuse me. I'm supposed to start work today." My thoughts were all over the place.

A blonde receptionist held up her hand and pointed to the phone that she held to her ears. Annoyed, but I masked it with a smile, as usual, while I waited patiently. Time was ticking. The blonde giggled and giggled, clearly wasting time. When she ended the call with *'love you honey'*, I realized it wasn't a work call. I checked the time again; the receptionist had taken up 4 minutes of my time chit-chatting with her lover. 7:59 AM.

"Be right back," said the receptionist, smiling. I felt like a fish out of the water.

"Hey, I just want…"

But I was speaking to the back side of the receptionist. I was boiling inside. When I looked in the mirror in the hall, I saw the hurt my cheeks were feeling was because there was a fake smile. I removed the smirk and looked around. People were going to their cubicles or walking around. There were a flight of stairs leading up to the mezzanine. I saw the receptionist going up there. My shoes pinched the sides of my feet, reminding me I had been standing too long. *This white girl deserved to be fired.*

After a few minutes, the receptionist came back.

"Hello, how may I help you?"

You can start by getting rid of your stupid head or pretending it actually works.

"I'm looking for Mr. Brown's office."

"Do you have an appointment?"

"I'm starting today."

"Oh, you're the new girl. You must be Gab…eh," the receptionist fucked my name up, blinking with her fake lashes.

"Gabrielle," I completed, almost flinching under the appraisal and hating myself for it.

The white girl has something against me, I was sure. Nothing about her fake attitude was welcoming.

"And you are?"

"Oh, I'm Anne. Listen, go up the stairs, the first door on the right is Mr. Brown's," she said, quickly dismissing me.

It was so abrupt that I stood looking at her, sizing her up. *She doesn't want none of this heat.* This was not a welcome party at all. Anne turned around and was already busy, doing her work. I quickly clambered up the stairs and paused once I got to the door.

"Deep breath, deep breath, deep breath. You're a strong black woman. You got this, sis!" I exhaled.

It was five minutes past 8. That damn white girl Anne made me late.

The door opened just as I raised my hand to knock. The little head of Mr. Brown stared at me from an imposing 6 feet.

"Oh, you," said Mr. Brown

"Gabrielle Muhammad."

"Gabriel. Your folks call females Gabriel?"

"Gabrielle, "I almost choked on what he said.

Brown shrugged, looking at his watch and then over at me.

"Anyway, come in and take a seat. I'll be back in a minute. I need a cup of coffee."

He went around me and disappeared. My mouth was open, and it was hard to close. I couldn't believe his racist ass talking about your folks. I sat down and waited for the tiny man to return. I would have bitten my fingernails if I hadn't got them done on the way up to Boston. The treatment I received so far was appalling. Even though I'm minutes into starting, I worried I had made a mistake and jumped too soon without looking.

"Okay, what do we have here?" Brown's brash voice irked its way down my ears. His lanky frame made him appear like someone who should be singing in an opera as a soprano.

"You're late, I see."

"The receptionist was too busy taking calls when I tried asking where in the building were you."

"Already chit-chatting with the receptionist, hey?"

"No, sir. I—"

"Well, listen, Gabriel…"

"Gabrielle."

"I know how the girls are around here. And believe me; chatting Anna on your very first day isn't something you'd like to be doing if it will make you late."

"I was not chatting with her, sir."

"Yes, we aren't causing global warming either. Anyway"

I wanted to scream. The words were already in my head that read - *Shut up, white boy! You got a loud mouth. Shut up before I shut you up!*

"I…um."

"Listen, Gabrielle, I really like you. I feel you can thrive here from what I see in your resume. So stay focus, ok?"

In the meantime, while he was talking, I wondered if his skin would peel off if he were struck by lightning. Some employees would lose it easily and even go as far as killing their employers.

"Yes, sir."

"Okay, I suppose you'd like to know where you will be stationed.

No, I'm don't, really. When I walked in, I saw 'that place over there is where I would be.'

"Come on and I'll show you," said Mr. Brown getting up and leading the way outside.

On the way to my work area, I noticed so many pairs of eyes looking at me. None were welcoming. They only looking me up and down.

"Good morning," I greeted a white woman who was sitting at the reception at the entrance of my work area.

She acted like she didn't hear me.

"Aw right? I'm going to just keep my mouth shut."

4

─────────

Three hours had passed and I couldn't wait for the day to end. There was nothing else that could further worsen the day. I caught my pants' fly open a full hour after going to the ladies' room. The eyes staring at me anytime I got up to get a file or run an office errand made me sick. All of my attempts at starting up any kind of conversation made me look a fool because nobody was interested. I felt silenced from the moment I got in the door. What made things worse was that my pants leg caught onto something underneath my desk and got ripped as I tried to free it.

I was nervous, making errors in my creation of media posts. It was time to regain focus and ignore the BS. Perhaps, I'll survive the first day.

The noon hour had finally hit after the morning crawled along at an excruciatingly pace. Finally, somebody came up to check on a sister.

"Hey, you're Gabrielle, right?"

I looked up from my cubicle to see a young man in his early thirties, smiling. His hairline was receding but I could still tell he was young.

"Yes," I replied, trying to put on a smile.

"I'm Harold. You came all the way from New York."

Okay, how did white boy know all of that?

"Yep…"

I did not know what to say afterward. Part of me wanted to say 'I'm busy' and end the conversation, while the other was reluctant to lose the first friendly person I had met in this place.

"I guess you can say that."

"Well, see you around. My cubicle is right down there," he said, pointing.

"O—kay!" I thought about how I would get home once my shift ended. With all these people's eyes on me, trying to find a blemish; with my torn pants and jittery body. I would just sit and wait for them to leave, then I would follow.

5

———

Gibbons had Pete trailing after him as they walked into a murder scene. He had shaken off the thoughts that had been beclouding him on the way and was now focused on the duty at hand. Gibs had to be because their lives depended on that focus which amounted to the difference between life and death.

"What do we have here?" he asked the first officer he met on the scene.

"Detective Gibbons?"

"Yes," Gibs responded holding up his badge. "And this my partner, Peter."

"Okay, I'm Sergeant Daniels. It would appear someone killed the victim with little of a fight, which is kind of baffling."

"How so?" asked Gibbons.

"Well, the table is facing the door. His

body is facing the same direction then if you look closely, you'll see a box stacked up by the window," the sergeant explained.

"From where he was sitting, he might have expected someone was coming. The door appears to be left unlocked."

"Perhaps he was sleep when the assailant came in?"

"Yeah, but that's a long shot."

The men walked inside the room, and Gibbons smelled the familiar coppery scent of blood. That scent still was fresh to him after all these years, but not Pete. Pete was new to homicide, only spending six months in division.

The dead man had a pen gripped tightly in his right hand and his head was on top of the files he had been working on before his death. The blood was drying up and gave another shade to the table's dark red vinyl. The flies were already soaked in blood.

"He had cameras in here, didn't he?" asked Gibbons.

"Um, the receptionist downstairs said he always had them off, and yesterday was no different."

"Who's he?" asked Pete.

"Mr. Morgan Brown, son of late business mogul, Octavius Lucious Brown. He's the owner of the new startup company here called Revival."

"The name Lucious? Who the hell would name their son that? What is he, Greek?"

"Don't know, sir."

"How about the cameras outside the door?"

"We've asked for the footage from the building manager. If you're ready, we can get it when we leave to go back to the station."

"Wait," Pete said, going around the body.

He lifted Brown's head gently and found a knife still stuck in the throat underneath his suit jacket.

"Gloves."

A detective standing by the door handed Pete a pair. Pete put them on and gently slipped out the knife. Then, he examined the neck. There was something that had been carved into the man's neck; something that had taken some precision.

"Black girl lover," Pete whispered.

6

It was 7:00 PM. I had waited for everyone to go home for the night. I buried my head into my desktop like my life depended on it. People were walking past me all day and I forced myself to not look up. It seemed like my co-workers' stares would never end. But finally when everyone seemed to have left, I stood up and grabbed my bag, using it to cover my torn pants. Time to go home and who knows if I'll be coming back.

I hadn't seen Mr. Brown come down to my cubicle since earlier. He probably was up there in his office working. Thinking of him made my cheeks hot as I thought back to the incident earlier in the morning. I wanted to handle my business and get something off my chest. We had to clear something out or at least come to some understanding. I'm not with the word *"folks"* nor did I like the way he character-assassinated me about Anne. As I grabbed the rails and going up the stairs, I felt my temperature rising. I was pissed and wanted to deal with somebody in here. There has to be some accountability. I reached the door of my employer and grabbed the doorknob but couldn't turn in. I stayed on it, meditating.

"Deep breath, deep breath," I exhaled.

I wanted to turn it and bulge inside his little office. We need to set the record straight that Anne had been a huge pain in my ass today and how does he dare to defend her. I'm no chump and I can't just let the man get away with what he allows to go on in this office.

I waited and waited and then coward up. I let go of the door handle. *What exactly was I hoping to achieve? I wondered. I thought I heard frantic movements behind the door, a cough, and then a bump.* I turned away and returned the way I came. Whatever the man was doing in the office was not my business. Maybe he was getting some.

No one was around in Revival's office building. When I got on the elevator, nobody boarded with me. The security guard at the front door sat and just looked at me. *Poor old man!* I didn't even say bye to him as I walked out. The only thing on my mind was finding a cab to take me back to Oak Hills.

"Taxi! Taxi!" I yelled. A driver pulled over and we were heading to the hotel. There was a pub along the way. I told the driver at the driver to let me out there. My body felt cold, like the cold hands of dread were trifling with my intestines. Something's wrong! But a hot drink would remove the coldness.

———

The pub wasn't big and had a lot of neon lights in the front. I expected it to be more people being that it was rush hour. However, in my present state, I'd rather it be empty.

"Rum, please. Without ice."

The bartender came back, and I gulped it down so fast that my throat was burning.

"Another glass, please."

"Are you okay?" asked the bartender as he poured.

"I really don't know."

I drank the second one, slower than the first.

"You must be new here? I haven't seen you around before."

"Is that a problem here?" I was feeling tipsy.

I whipped my hair to get rid of the strands blocking my view.

"No, no. I'm Andre. What's your name, honey?"

"Gabrielle." *How this white boy got a black boy name, I wondered.*

"Gabrielle, your skin is so radiant."

"That's the first line I've heard?"

Andre chuckled watching me for sometime before he asked, "What's on your mind? You look stressed."

"You won't understand."

"Why because I'm white?"

"Oh, you know, then. Pour me another drink."

"One thing you fail to realize," said Andre as he poured. "Is that there's black in all the white and there's white in all the black?"

"Whatever."

"You had a rough day. Most of the customers laugh at my jokes. Let's talk about it?" He looked genuine. This little white boy is sweet.

"Nah, I'm good. I don't want to talk about it."

Andre went to serve someone else, starting up a conversation and talking to death. I wished it was that easy for me here. While Andre was busy chatting, it was my signal to bounce up out. It's getting dark, and I had to get back the hotel before the lynch mob shows up.

"Leaving already?" Andre called after me, realizing I was leaving.

I turned around and glanced at the table to make sure I hadn't forgotten to drop any extra bills.

"Come around again. We can talk about whatever."

"I'll see."

———

It took me 15 minutes to get back to the hotel. The bellboy kept looking at me like I was a rare exhibit, and even Billy, the receptionist whose name tag was falling off. They responded nonchalantly to my hello. I got to the first floor and put the keys in the door. The tiredness in my eyes overwhelming me. I need sleep. The key turned smoothly in the lock, clicking the door open. Once I shut it and walked in, I sensed someone behind me inside.

"Welcome, Miss. Gabrielle," Gibbons announced.

"Who.. who the hell are you?"

"Detective Gibbons at your service."

"I don't remember calling the police."

"I'm sure you don't. I'd like to take you in for questioning."

"What's this about? You can't just walk into my room…! Who gave you the key, anyway?!"

"Your employer, Mr. Brown's dead."

"My employer is… what? What did you say?"

"Mr. Brown's dead."

"No, don't play with me! What the hell do you want with me then?"

"We were wondering if you can come with me and my partner, Pete to help us clarify some things."

"Brown's dead… dead?"

"Yes."

"Let me go change and I'll be right out. Oh my God!"

———

During the drive to the police station, I was quiet and rebuffed every attempt Gibbons made to engage with me in a conversation. They escorted me to an empty room with a steel table. I asked was I under arrest. They told me that as of now; we are looking at potential suspects without giving me a direct answer.

"You're the only black employee at Revival, is that right?" asked Gibbons.

I sighed. Why does everything have to be about color? I shifted my gaze over to Gibbons' partner, Pete. His face spelled all the letters of impatience. I don't like him.

"I don't really know. Today was my first day. I was at my cubicle all day."

"Were you discriminated against anytime during your day at work?"

"Yeah, you can say that."

"Is that why you did it?" Pete interrupted. "You were tired of taking those crackers' shit? Weren't you?"

"Hmm. I just started working there. I don't know what you're talking about?

"Well, you thought about it all day how to get back at Mr. Brown. You were tired of those white people looking at you like a piece of shit. Weren't you?" added Pete.

"I don't know what you're talking about, sir."

"You killed Mr. Brown, didn't you? You waited till everyone was gone, then went upstairs to kill him."

"Why would I do that? The man just hired me."

I looked at Gibbons and wanted to know what was going on behind his hooded eyes.

"Everyone we've talked to at Revival felt you didn't deserve the job. You were making errors and in and out of the bathroom all day."

"That's my business. Again, I have no reason to kill Mr. Brown. I only saw the man once today when he took me to my desk."

"Who does this knife belong to then?"

The knife that Pete produced, was thrown on the table in an evidence bag.

"What? I've never seen this knife in my life."

"Well, it has your prints on it," persisted Pete.

I shook my head, not believing a word they were saying. They must have seen the video which showed me sneaking up to Mr. Brown's office. They were trying to pressure me to give a confession. Well, at least Pete was. I don't think the other detective, Gibbons, believed I killed Mr. Brown. He had such kind eyes but looks are deceiving.

"I have not touched that knife in my life," I said. Maybe Gibbons would believe me. He sat quietly, letting Pete, carry on with the interrogation. The man looked like it was of any use. I didn't do it, and I think he knew it.

"Miss. Gabrielle, where were you from 7:15 pm to 7:30 pm this evening."

I thought over and over about where I was being careful to answer. "In the bar, pub, tavern whatever y'all call it here down the street a few blocks away from the company's building. I was talking with a bartender, named Andre the whole time. I think that's his name."

"A black bartender in Boston? You're lying, young lady?" said Pete.

"I know the kid, Pete. He's a white boy

with a black name." Gibbons exhaled in relief.

Detective Gibbons suddenly appeared handsome in my eyes. Maybe under different circumstances, we could have see where it would go but not tonight.

"You can go home for now. But don't leave town until we contact you. We may have more questions."

"Yes, sir."

7

Back at Oak Hills Hotel, I stared out the window. The streets were empty, and the nightfall shielded the sidewalks. I had a heavy heart waiting in anticipation about what will happen next. I couldn't leave town, and Detective Pete kept reminding me that if I did before they called, they can arrest me for obstruction of justice.

I was tired. My eyes followed the cars as they raced each other up the street. My gaze went to the phone near the desk in the room. I needed to talk to Ummi. She was the only one that could calm me down. The phone rang for a long time before someone answered.

"Hello, salaam alaikum."

"Hello, Ummi. It's me, wa alaikum as salaam." I sniffed feeling cold.

"How are you?"

"I'm not good, mom. I'm losing it. The police accused me of murder but they believe my alibi."

"What! "What the hell are you talking about girl? Stop being silly."

"It's true, Ummi. Someone killed my boss."

"When?

"Tonight, they took me in for questioning, but they are checking out my alibi."

"Come back to New York now, Gabrielle. I'll call your father. He's at work."

"I can't yet. The detectives said I can't leave Boston. They also said that my fingerprints were found on the murder weapon. I don't know how."

"Oh, Lord have mercy. Please make dua!"

I heard Ummi talking to a male probably my dad. I wasn't trying to make him upset.

"Mom, I'll call you back."

"Gabrielle, wait. Your sister wants to talk to you."

"I'll call tomorrow. Tell Khadi I miss her. Everything will be okay, I hope."

"Masalama."

I walked to the window again, struggling to control my emotions. I was shaking and was about to cry.

———

Meanwhile, it suddenly hit Detective Gibbons just as he was going late night grocery shopping. There was something he and Pete had overlooked. He knew that Gabrielle was not the murderer but couldn't let her off the hook unless someone else emerged as a suspect. He called Pete once he got home.

"I have something. We need to look at the video footage again."

"What the hell, Gibs. It's 2 AM. I'm sleeping with my babe."

"Meet me at the squad room in thirty minutes and make sure you bring coffee and donuts."

With the grocery shopping completely off Gib's mind, he sped the car towards the station forgetting everything he bought.

Detective Gibbons got back to the precinct in ten minutes and sat in his car into the police's parking lot for a few minutes. Exhaling, he slowly walked through the precinct's doors. There were a few uniformed guys on duty, sipping coffee waiting for calls for the night.

"Hey Bob," Gibbons greeted the eldest officer on the floor.

"Come to join us for night shift?"

"You wish, you cocksucker."

Gibbons walked to the back of the precinct to the video room where he checked out the log and took the footage labeled "Revival Murder." He slotted it into the computer's DVD drive while the officer went up front. He rewound it to the beginning and watched. The camera focused only on the front of the office door. As he were watching, Pete came in and joined him.

"What is this all about, Gibs? Getting me out of the bed of one of my honies."

"Fucking dickhead. Just watch. So far, everyone is entering and leaving Mr. Brown's office throughout the day."

"Is that supposed to be the damn nightly news?"

They sat for nearly twenty minutes while Pete was nearly falling asleep until Gibbons rewound it back a little after spotting something.

"Wake up, Pete. See this guy."

"Yeah?"

The person had a reclining hairline and was smiling.

"He never came out after 6:30 PM."

They re-watched the footage from beginning to end and concluded that the reclining-hairline guy never came out of the office.

"How did the hell did he leave then? We watched the tape all the way until we came," asked Pete.

"The window, perhaps."

"We need to call for the street camera footage. We've got our guy."

I stared at the TV with empty eyes. I took me awhile to realize the buzzer was ringing. I didn't know that hotel rooms had them. I hurried. Detective Gibbons was there, looking like a cast out of a movie. It was 5:09 AM.

"Sorry for disturbing you. I had to tell you in person you're free to go."

"I am?"

"Yes, can I come in?"

"Sure." Detective Gibbons stood there, not sure of how to proceed further.

"Wanna a cup of coffee?"

"No, thanks. Just listen up. I won't be long. It turns out that the murderer is a guy name Harold. Do you know him?"

"We've met."

"Did he shake your hands with gloves on?"

"Maybe. I don't know. Hmm, I think so."

"That may explain the fingerprints on the knife. We got them off the gloves he wore."

"Are you sure?"

"I believe so. He went inside Mr. Brown's office when he stepped out for lunch and was there, waiting until everyone went home. The street camera caught him climbing out of Mr. Brown's window around the time of the murder."

"Why the hell would he kill that poor man?"

"Apparently, we found out that Harold was fucking with Mr. Brown's wife and wanted to get rid of him before he found out. Excuse my French. Your arrival was his chance he couldn't afford to miss."

I tried digesting all of this with little success.

"Well, I'll be going now," said Gibbons, walking towards the door.

Deep down inside, I wanted to stop him from leaving and I could tell he didn't want to take off either. If I wasn't Muslim, I'd tell him to come chill with me for the night.

While at the door, Gibbons asked, "Will you still be staying in town?"

"I don't know yet," I replied already knowing since Ummi told me to come back, I'd be on the first thing going to New York in the morning.

"Well, take my card. Maybe we can have some lunch one of these days. You know?"

"Yeah, right? Not today, Gibs. I'm Muslim and I can't just be hanging out with boys like that."

"Oh, I forgot to mention that you may be subpoenaed in court as a witness when we catch Harold for the murder trial. I'm sorry. It's standard procedure."

"Oh my God! Why me?"

Detective Gibbons left smiling, walking through the corridor with a schoolboy swagger like he got one on his way to his squad car.

I started packing, knowing for sure, it was time to go. Hey! I got a good life in my room at Abee and Ummi's house. Sometimes, you have to just reset and thank Allah for another day.

ABOUT THE AUTHOR

Eric Reese was born and raised in Philadelphia, Pennsylvania , USA and is the recipient of the first Mayoral Scholarship of Philadelphia (1993) and the Philadelphia Federation of Teachers Human Relations Award (1989).

Enjoyed the story?

Kindly review it and read the second episode!

www.ingramcontent.com/pod-product-compliance
Lightning Source LLC
Chambersburg PA
CBHW051301190726

48286CB00004B/1212